CALENDAR CLUB

The Case of

NEW YEAR'S EVE NIGHTMARE

MVFOL

by **NANCY STAR**

Illustrated by
JAMES BERNARDIN

SCHOLASTIC INC.

New York Toronto London Auckland Sydney
Mexico City New Delhi Hong Kong Buenos Aires

To Jane, with love
—N. S.

To my friends Emily and Andrew Cline
—J. B.

ISBN 0-439-67265-1

Text copyright © 2005 by Nancy Star
Illustrations copyright © 2005 by Scholastic Inc.
All rights reserved. Published by Scholastic Inc.

SCHOLASTIC and associated logos are trademarks
and/or registered trademarks of Scholastic Inc.

12 11 10 9 8 7   14 15 16/0

Printed in the U.S.A.
First printing, December 2005

Book design by Jennifer Rinaldi Windau

CHAPTER ONE

NIGHTMARES ON DAISY LANE!

"Do you want to hear about the nightmare I had last night?" asked Casey.

Casey Calendar sat on her front steps eating cookies with her best friends, Dottie Plum and Leon Spector.

"I had a nightmare last night, too," said Dottie.

"So did I," said Leon. "But I can't remember it."

He glanced at Ginger, Dottie's cat.

Ginger was a cat who thought she was a dog. She was also a cat who loved cookies.

Ginger stared at Leon's cookie, hoping for a crumb.

"Now I remember," Leon said. "Ginger was in my nightmare!"

"She was in mine, too!" said Dottie.

"Was Ginger wearing a burglar's mask in your nightmare?" asked Casey.

"Yes!" Dottie and Leon said together.

Dottie, Casey, and Leon had started the Calendar Club together. They solved mysteries together. But they had never had a nightmare together before.

Just then, a delivery truck pulled up in front of Casey's house.

Two men got out. The driver was tall. His helper was short.

The short man opened the back of the truck. He unloaded twenty folding chairs onto the driveway.

"Where do you want these?" he asked.

"Are the chairs for the party?" Casey asked.

"Yes," said the man.

"The party is at Number One Daisy Lane." Dottie pointed to her house.

Tonight was Dottie's parents' annual New Year's Eve party. Dottie, Casey, and Leon wanted to go, but they weren't invited.

The men loaded the chairs back on the truck. "I told you to check the address," the tall man told the short man.

Mrs. List, who lived two houses down, came outside to see what was going on.

"Are those chairs for the party tonight?" Mrs. List asked the three friends.

"Yes," said Dottie. "But they delivered them to Casey's house by mistake."

The delivery men got back in the truck. They drove next door to Dottie's house. They started unloading again.

Ginger rubbed against Casey's leg. That reminded Casey about their nightmare.

"Mrs. List," said Casey. "Did you ever hear of three people having the same nightmare?"

Casey always asked a lot of questions, but Mrs. List didn't mind. She was a teacher at the Fruitvale Elementary School. She was used to questions.

"We all dreamed Ginger was a burglar," explained Leon.

Mrs. List thought for a moment. "Has the Calendar Club been trying to help find the Fruitvale Cat Burglar?" she asked.

"Yes," said Dottie.

"That might explain it," said Mrs. List. "Sometimes people dream about things at night that they were thinking about during the day."

"Do you think we dreamed the cat was a burglar because we were thinking about the cat burglar?" asked Casey.

"Maybe," said Mrs. List. "You do know cat burglars aren't really cats, don't you?"

"Yes," said Leon. "They're just burglars who sneak around in the dark."

"Did you know they're called cat burglars because they move as quietly as cats?" asked Casey.

"Yes," said Mrs. List. "But I don't know what the Fruitvale Cat Burglar has stolen."

"I can tell you that," said Dottie. She took her notebook out of her back pocket.

Dottie carried her notebook wherever she went. Inside, she kept lists. Her favorite list was of the weather.

"Today," Dottie's list said, "is the warmest New Year's Eve in fifty years."

She turned to the page called "Fruitvale Cat Burglar." She read out loud.

"The Fruitvale Cat Burglar has stolen watches, money, and jewelry. He likes diamond jewelry best."

"Officer Gill told us that," Leon said. "We've been helping him look for clues."

"Maybe you'll find some clues at the party tonight," said Mrs. List. "There'll be lots of people there."

"It's a grown-ups-only party," said Dottie. "We're having a sleepover at Casey's house instead."

"I'm sure that will be fun, too," said Mrs. List.

The delivery men finished carrying the chairs into Dottie's house.

"Happy New Year," they called as they got in their truck.

"Happy New Year," everyone called back.

Mrs. List went home. Dottie, Casey, and Leon took Ginger for a walk.

They were halfway up the block when Warren Bunn and his best friend, Derek Fleck, pulled up behind them on their bikes.

Warren Bunn was a boy in their grade who was a bully and proud of it.

"Lose someone?" asked Warren.

Dottie and Casey looked around. Leon was nowhere to be seen.

This was nothing new.

Leon was a collector. His favorite collection was of rocks in the shapes of states. Leon hoped someday he would have an entire map of the United States made out of rocks.

But sometimes Leon wandered off. So while Leon was looking for rocks, Dottie and Casey were looking for Leon.

"What's up with Leon?" Warren asked. "Is he looking for rocks in the shape of cat burglars?"

"What do you know about cat burglars?" asked Casey.

"Maybe I am a cat burglar," said Warren. "Maybe I just snuck into your house and stole all your stuff."

"Yeah," said Derek. "Maybe I helped."

Just then Leon ran out from behind a tree in front of Mrs. List's house.

"I found something," he said. He joined his friends.

"What is it?" asked Warren. "A pile of diamonds?"

Derek laughed so hard he fell down on the ground.

"Just a rock," Leon said. He kept his hands behind his back.

"Let me see it," Warren said.

"How did you know the burglar likes diamonds?" Casey asked, to change the subject.

"Maybe I'm the burglar," said Derek. "Maybe I have diamonds in my pockets." He started to laugh again.

"That's not funny," Warren snapped.

Derek stopped laughing.

Warren got on his bike and rode off.

"Wait up," Derek yelled. He got on his bike and rode after his friend.

"What did you find?" Casey asked Leon once the bullies were gone.

"This," said Leon. He held up a shiny black cloth sack.

"Are you going to use it to keep rocks in?" asked Casey.

"No," said Leon.

"Why not?" asked Casey.

"I think I know," said Dottie.

She opened her notebook and read aloud. "Cat burglars usually dress in black so they can't be seen in the dark."

"Which means they probably carry a black bag, too," said Leon.

He glanced up the block. "Look." He pointed.

Officer Gill was standing in front of a neighbor's house, talking.

"Come on," said Casey. "Let's show Officer Gill what you found."

CHAPTER TWO

THE BLACK SACK!

Dottie, Casey, and Leon waited while Officer Gill finished talking to their neighbor, Mrs. Foust.

"You're all set," Officer Gill told Mrs. Foust.

"I'm sorry to be a bother," said Mrs. Foust.

"It's never a bother to check things out," said Officer Gill.

"Happy New Year," said Mrs. Foust to Officer Gill. She went inside her house.

"Is everything okay?" Casey asked.

"Yes," said Officer Gill. "Mrs. Foust came home and found a window open. But it turns out Mr. Foust opened it because he wanted some fresh air."

Officer Gill noticed Leon was holding something in his hand.

"What do you have there?" he asked.

"I found something," Leon said. He handed over the black sack.

"We think it might belong to the cat burglar," said Dottie.

Officer Gill examined the sack carefully.

"We were wondering what the cat burglar used to carry away his loot," said Officer Gill. "I think you may have found it."

Officer Gill took his notebook out of his back pocket.

Dottie took her notebook out of her back pocket.

"Where exactly did you find this?" asked Officer Gill.

"Come on," said Casey. "We'll show you."

The three friends led Officer Gill to Mrs. List's front yard. Leon walked over to the big tree.

"I found it right here," he said.

Officer Gill, Dottie, Casey, and Leon studied the ground for clues.

Casey pointed to a spot behind the tree. There were marks in the dirt. "Are those footprints?"

Officer Gill looked closely. "It looks like a lot of footprints," he said.

"Could there be a lot of cat burglars?" Casey asked.

"I'm not sure," said Officer Gill. "We'll have to check that out. And we'll have to check this out." He held up the sack. "Thanks for bringing it to me. Will I see you later at the party?"

"Why are the police going to the party?" asked Casey.

Officer Gill laughed. "I'm off duty tonight. I'm going as a guest. But I won't be going at all if I don't get down to the station house soon. See you later." He headed to his patrol car and drove away.

"I didn't know Officer Gill was going to be at the party," said Dottie.

Now they wanted to go even more.

"Did you remind your mom that tomorrow is your birthday?" Casey asked. "Maybe she'll let us come because of your birthday."

"I tried that," Dottie said.

"What did she say?" asked Casey.

"She didn't say anything," said Dottie. "She was too busy thinking about New Year's Eve party hats and noisemakers."

"What if we tell her we found the cat burglar's black sack?" asked Casey. "What if we tell her we need to go to the party on official Calendar Club business? She can't say no to that!"

Dottie thought her mother could definitely say no to that.

But she didn't get a chance to say so.

Casey had already run to Dottie's house to ask Mrs. Plum herself.

CHAPTER THREE

A NOTE!

`Mrs. Plum was` in the dining room
putting party hats and noisemakers on
the table.

"Would you like some noisemakers?"
she asked when the three friends walked
into the room. "I have extras."

"Thanks," said Dottie. She picked a
tasseled trumpet.

Casey took a silver horn. Leon chose a metal cowbell.

They put the noisemakers in their pockets.

"Mrs. Plum," Casey said, "can we please come to your New Year's Eve party?"

"You're going to have your own party," said Mrs. Plum. "You'll love your new babysitter, Miss Grace."

"But we want to go to your party," said Dottie. "We might find clues about the cat burglar."

"The cat burglar is not invited to my party," said Mrs. Plum. "And you can come later. We asked Miss Grace to bring you over at midnight to say hello. If you're still awake."

"You say we can come at midnight every year," said Dottie. "But we always fall asleep."

"Maybe this year will be different," said

Mrs. Plum. She checked her watch. "You'd better go. Miss Grace will be at Casey's house soon."

Dottie, Casey, and Leon left. They stopped in Casey's backyard to check the Calendar Club Help Box.

The Help Box was right outside the Calendar Clubhouse door. Dottie, Casey, and Leon took turns checking it every day.

Dottie kept a tally in her notebook to keep track of whose turn it was to check next.

"It's your turn, Leon," said Dottie. She looked up from her notebook. "Leon?"

Leon came running up the gravel driveway.

"Sorry," he said. "I thought I found a rock of New York."

"Why are you looking for New York?" asked Casey.

"Because Times Square is in New York

City," said Leon. "And people have been watching the ball drop in Times Square on New Year's Eve for over one hundred years."

Leon knew lots of facts like that. His friends were used to it.

He looked inside the Help Box. "There's a note!" he called out.

Leon took out the note and read it out loud.

Dear Calendar Club,
I just wanted to say hello! I can't wait to meet you! From your new babysitter,
Miss Isabelle Grace.

The Calendar Club liked getting notes from people who needed help. But they were disappointed to get a note that just said hello.

"I don't like new babysitters very much," said Dottie.

"She might be nice," said Leon.

They walked down Casey's driveway.

"Do you think if she's nice she'll let us stay in the clubhouse all night?" asked Casey.

"No," said Leon. "Not with the Fruitvale Cat Burglar on the loose."

They sat on Casey's front steps and waited for Miss Grace.

After awhile, they saw a woman walking down the block.

"Is that her?" asked Casey.

The woman was very small. She had short blond hair. As she got closer, they saw she carried two large shopping bags. The bags were almost as big as she was.

The woman arrived at Casey's front walk just as a delivery truck drove by.

The men who dropped off the chairs were making another delivery.

"Happy New Year," they called from their truck.

"Happy New Year," the friends called back.

The babysitter joined them.

"Don't you just love New Year's Eve?" she asked.

The three friends nodded. They felt a little shy.

"I forgot to introduce myself," said the woman. "I'm Isabelle Grace. At your service." Miss Grace bowed.

"Let's go inside," she said, "and tell your mother I'm here."

They walked into the house. Miss Grace handed one of her bags to Dottie.

"Can you put this somewhere safe?" she asked. "It's very important."

She handed the other bag to Casey. "Can you put this in the basement? We'll go there in a little while."

"Why do you want to go to the

basement?" asked Casey. "What's in the bags? Why is that one so important?"

"You ask a lot of questions," said Miss Grace.

Casey went to put the bag in the basement.

"I've got some ideas for games to play," said Miss Grace when Casey returned. "And some fun projects for us to do."

"Do you mind if we go to our clubhouse for a little while first?" Casey asked.

"We have a club," said Dottie. "We solve mysteries."

"Right now we're working on the case of the Fruitvale Cat Burglar," Leon explained.

"It's almost New Year's Eve. Let's not talk about the cat burglar," said Miss Grace. "Okay?"

They nodded. But they did not know why Miss Grace wasn't interested in hearing about the cat burglar.

"I know what we'll do," said Miss Grace. "We'll start by making our very own noisemakers."

"Do we have to make noisemakers?" Casey asked. "We already have some."

Before Miss Grace could answer, Casey's parents came down the stairs. They were all dressed up and ready to go to the party.

"Are you having fun with your new babysitter?" asked Mrs. Calendar.

"We're having lots of fun," said Miss Grace before anyone else could answer. "We're going to make noisemakers now. Later, I'll show them how to do cartwheels."

"Wonderful!" said Mr. Calendar.

"We already know how to do cartwheels," said Dottie.

"You'd better get going," Miss Grace told Casey's parents. "The party's already started."

"Can we please come?" asked Casey.

"Don't be silly," said Miss Grace. "We're going to have a wonderful time right here."

Miss Grace held open the front door.

Mr. and Mrs. Calendar gave Casey a kiss.

"Be good," said Mrs. Calendar as she walked outside.

"I'm sure they will be," said Miss Grace. She gave Casey's parents a big, wide smile.

She waved as they walked down the path toward Dottie's house.

Then she closed the door.

The smile disappeared from her face.

Suddenly, the friendly babysitter didn't look very friendly at all.

CHAPTER FOUR

QUIET AS A CAT!

Miss Grace looked around the living room. "Maybe I should close the blinds," she said.

"Why?" asked Casey.

"Privacy," said Miss Grace.

"I can see my house through those windows," Dottie said. "I like to see my house."

Miss Grace looked out the window at Dottie's house. The curtains at Dottie's house were closed.

"All right," said Miss Grace. "I'll leave the blinds open. Where's the basement?"

Casey led them to the basement door, in the kitchen.

Miss Grace opened the door. She

peered down the dark stairs. "Is there a light?"

The light switch was at the top of the stairs. Casey turned it on.

The basement looked dark even with the light on.

"Let's go down," said Miss Grace.

"Why?" asked Casey.

"To work on our projects," said Miss Grace.

"Why can't we do our projects in the living room?" asked Casey. "My mom lets us work there. We're always neat and careful."

"Glue and glitter do not belong in the living room," said Miss Grace.

"Can we do it here?" asked Casey. "At the kitchen table?"

Miss Grace sighed. She walked over to the windows. The windows faced the backyard.

"I guess these windows are all right," she said. "We'll work here. Now where is my bag?"

"Here," said Leon. He pointed to the bag next to him.

"I meant the bag I gave to you," Miss Grace said to Casey. "That one has the glitter, glue, and noisemaker supplies."

"We already have noisemakers," said Dottie for the second time.

"I'll make noisemakers, then," said Miss Grace. "You can make confetti. Now where is that bag?"

"You asked me to put it in the basement," said Casey. "Remember?"

"Right," said Miss Grace. "I'll get it."

Miss Grace went down the basement stairs.

"Why does she care so much about windows?" asked Casey.

"I don't know," said Dottie.

"What's in that bag?" Casey asked. She pointed to the bag next to Leon. "That's the one she said was important."

Leon glanced into the bag. "There's a big jar of glue on top," he said.

Casey walked to the top of the stairs and called down to Miss Grace. "Miss Grace. The glue is in the bag up here."

"Thank you," said Miss Grace. "I'll be there in a second. I'm just getting everything organized. You may take the glue out of that bag," she added.

Leon started to take the glue out of the bag. Then he saw something that made him gasp.

"What is it?" asked Casey.

He took out the glue. Then he pointed to what was underneath. Casey and Dottie looked.

Dottie saw it first. "A mask!"

"That's the kind of mask Ginger wore in my dream," Leon said.

"Is it a cat burglar mask?" Casey asked. Then she noticed something else. "What's that?"

She got a flashlight. Dottie shined it in.

"It's a necklace," Leon said.

"Is it a diamond necklace?" Casey asked.

"If it's a real diamond necklace and a real burglar's mask," Dottie said, "does that mean Miss Grace is a real — "

"I'm real all right," Miss Grace interrupted.

The three friends looked up. Casey put the flashlight behind her back so Miss Grace couldn't see it.

"We didn't hear you come up the stairs," said Leon.

"Did anyone ever tell you you're quiet as a cat?" asked Casey.

"Or a cat burglar," whispered Dottie.

CHAPTER FIVE
THE TRAP

"This is going to be harder than I thought," said Miss Grace to herself.

She looked at the clock. "It's only eight-thirty. The best thing to do is just get started.

"Come, sit down," she said to the three friends.

Dottie, Casey, and Leon sat down at the table.

Miss Grace put out jars of glue, glitter, and paint. She laid out scissors, colored paper, magazines, cups, and ribbon.

"What's all this for?" asked Casey.

"To keep you busy," said Miss Grace.

"Why do you want to keep us busy?" asked Casey.

"You ask a lot of questions, don't you?" said Miss Grace.

Miss Grace looked at her jacket. It was very fancy. It was covered with beads and sequins. "I had better take this off," she said. "I don't want to get glue and glitter on it."

She took off her jacket.

"What are you staring at?" she asked the three friends. "Haven't you ever seen someone wearing a black sweater and black pants before?"

She went to hang up her jacket in the hall closet.

Dottie took out her notebook and turned to her cat burglar list.

"She's wearing all black clothes," Dottie said, checking her list. "She has a mask and a diamond necklace in her bag. And she walks as quietly as a cat."

"Do you think she really could be the Fruitvale Cat Burglar?" asked Casey.

"She might be," said Leon.

"But we don't know for sure," said Dottie.

"What if we put something valuable on the table?" Casey asked. "Then we can leave the room and see what happens. If she takes it, we'll know for sure."

"That's a great idea," said Dottie.

"What's a great idea?" asked Miss Grace.

They jumped up, startled. They hadn't heard Miss Grace walk in.

"It would be a great idea if we wore smocks," said Dottie. "So we don't get glue on our clothes, either."

"That *is* a good idea," said Miss Grace.

The three friends raced up to Casey's room.

"What do I have that's valuable?" Casey asked as they looked around.

Her shelves were filled with books, stuffed animals, and photographs.

Leon picked something up. "What about this?"

He held a small jade cupid in his hand. Their neighbor, Ms. Duffy, had given it to Casey as a gift.

"That's perfect," said Dottie.

"But what if she really takes it?" Casey asked. She loved her jade cupid.

"We'll go get Officer Gill," said Leon. "And he'll get it back."

"Okay," Casey agreed.

"We need to distract Miss Grace while we put the cupid on the table," said Dottie.

"I have an idea," said Casey.

They went back to the kitchen.

"Can you please make us some hot chocolate?" Casey asked.

"Okay," said Miss Grace.

"I'll show you where the cocoa mix is," said Casey.

Miss Grace followed Casey to the pantry closet. The pantry closet was big enough to walk inside.

"It's up there," Casey said.

Leon quickly put the jade cupid on the table near Miss Grace's seat.

Miss Grace came out with the cocoa mix. She made them hot chocolate. Then she sat back down.

"Oh, no," said Dottie. "We forgot to get smocks."

"Hurry up and get them," said Miss Grace.

Dottie, Casey, and Leon left the room. But they didn't go right upstairs. They stayed and peeked into the kitchen to watch.

Miss Grace sat for a few seconds. She noticed the jade cupid. She reached for it.

The three friends ran upstairs to find smocks.

They came back down wearing Casey's father's old shirts.

They sat down at the kitchen table and stared.

The jade cupid was gone!

CHAPTER SIX

THE GREAT ESCAPE

Miss Grace was making a noisemaker.

"Why don't you get started on that confetti," she said.

Dottie, Casey, and Leon took several sheets of shiny gold and silver paper. They started cutting.

"I'm done," said Leon. He pushed his pile of confetti toward Miss Grace.

"I'm done, too," said Dottie.

"You're quick," said Miss Grace. She put all of the confetti in a cup.

"I'm done," said Casey. "Is it midnight yet? Can we go to the party now?"

"So many questions!" said Miss Grace. She pointed to the clock on the wall. "It's only nine o'clock. It's too early to go to the party."

"Would you mind if Dottie, Leon, and I went up to my room for a little while?" Casey asked sweetly.

"All right," Miss Grace said. She stood up and walked over to her bag. She reached inside.

The three friends froze. They didn't know what she would pull out.

Miss Grace took a book out of her bag.

She followed them to the stairs. She turned and locked the top lock on the front door.

The top lock was too high for Dottie, Casey, or Leon to reach.

"You can go up," said Miss Grace. "I'll be in the living room, reading."

The three friends ran up the steps as fast as they could.

"We can use the phone in my parents'

room to call Officer Gill," Casey whispered
when they got to the top of the stairs.

They ran to her parents' phone. Casey
picked up the receiver. But there was no
dial tone. The phone didn't work.

"We've got to get help," said Leon.

"Why don't we go out the back door?"
Casey asked. "Miss Grace didn't double-
lock that one."

They tiptoed down the stairs.

Casey pointed to all the creaky spots so
no one would step on them.

They crept to the living room and peeked inside.

Miss Grace was sitting in a chair, reading a book called *Stealing for Fun*.

They continued on to the kitchen.

Casey got the flashlight from the shelf. Leon carefully unlocked the back door and opened it.

Dottie went out first. Casey came next. Leon, as always, came last.

They hurried across the backyard.

Leon stopped and bent down to pick something up.

"Leon!" Dottie said. "This is not the time to look for rocks."

"Drop it," a man's voice called out.

Leon stuffed the rock into his pocket.

They looked around. They didn't see anyone.

"I said *don't* drop it this time!" the voice called out again.

Dottie saw them first. She pointed. Then they all saw.

Two men were standing near the bushes between Casey and Dottie's houses.

There was a full moon, so there was a lot of light. But it was still hard to see the men because they were dressed all in black.

One man was very tall. The other man was very short. The short man carried a black sack. And they were both wearing masks!

CHAPTER SEVEN
MASKED MEN!

"That sack looks just like the one I found," whispered Leon.

"Their masks look just like the one in Miss Grace's bag," whispered Dottie.

"Aren't those the men who delivered the chairs?" asked Casey.

"Yes," said Dottie.

"Do you think they're Miss Grace's partners?" whispered Casey.

"We need to get Officer Gill," said Dottie.

"How are we going to get past them?" asked Casey.

"What did you say, Lou?" asked the tall man.

"I didn't say anything, Pat," said the short man.

"Quick," Casey whispered. "Let's hide in the clubhouse."

They ran across the lawn and ducked into the clubhouse.

They could hear the cat burglars arguing.

"Make sure you don't lose the bag this time," said Pat.

"I wasn't the one who dropped it last time," said Lou. "And why am I the one who has to climb through the windows?"

"Do I look like I could fit?" asked Pat. "You're the climber. I'm the brains. Get it?"

"Can't we go in through a door just once?" asked Lou.

"People don't usually leave their doors wide open," said Pat. "Now let's get back to the plan. You're going into the back

bedroom. All the guests' purses will be on the bed. Grab as many as you can."

"How will I know which one is the back bedroom?" Lou asked.

Pat grabbed the black sack from Lou and bopped Lou on the head.

"It's the room with the coats on the bed, you ding-dong," said Pat. "You can see it from here." Pat pointed toward Dottie's house. "See those pink walls."

"That's my bedroom," Dottie whispered to her friends.

"What did you say?" asked Pat.

"I didn't say anything," said Lou.

Dottie and Casey put their hands over their mouths to make sure they didn't say anything else.

Leon took his hand out of his pocket to do the same thing. But when he took his hand out of his pocket, a rock clattered to the floor.

"I heard that," said Lou.

Pat pulled a flashlight out of his pocket. He shined the light around the yard. He saw the clubhouse.

"What's that?" he asked.

"A doghouse," said Lou.

Pat was scared of dogs. "What kind of dog needs a house that big?"

"A big dog," said Lou.

Lou pointed the flashlight toward Casey's open back door.

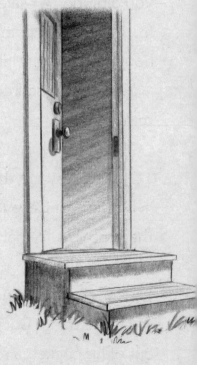

"Look," said Lou. "That door is wide open." He walked to the door and listened.

"No one's home," said Lou. "We can do two jobs in one night."

"Okay," said Pat. "Let's do it."

The burglars walked in the house.

The friends ran out of the clubhouse.

"Miss Grace isn't the Fruitvale Cat Burglar!" said Leon.

"We've got to warn her," said Dottie.

"Come on," said Casey. "I've got an idea."

CHAPTER EIGHT
TO THE RESCUE!

Dottie and Leon followed Casey to the side of her house.

They all looked through the living room window.

Miss Grace was sitting in the chair. Her eyes were closed. Her book was on her lap, upside down.

"She's sleeping," said Leon.

"Not for long," said Casey.

She tapped on the window. But Miss Grace didn't wake up.

She tried to open the window. But it was stuck.

"Let's try it together," said Dottie.

On the count of three, they lifted the window open.

They were about to call to Miss Grace. Then they saw the cat burglars tiptoe past the living room.

The burglars didn't notice Miss Grace. They went up the stairs to the second floor.

"Hurry," said Casey. "We've got to help Miss Grace."

Dottie slipped in through the window first. Casey came next. Leon, as always, was last.

"Miss Grace," Dottie whispered. "Wake up."

Miss Grace opened her eyes.

"There are two cat burglars upstairs," said Casey. "We've got to get help. Come on. We can go out the back door."

Miss Grace didn't ask any questions. She followed the three friends to the kitchen.

Then they heard footsteps running down the stairs.

"Let's hide," said Casey. "Over there."
She pointed to the kitchen pantry. "We can
all fit inside," she said.

Casey grabbed several jars of glitter, glue,
and confetti from the table.

"Just in case," she explained as they
squeezed into the pantry closet.

She pulled the door closed. It was still
open a crack when Pat and Lou walked into
the kitchen.

"What's down there?" Lou asked, pointing the flashlight toward the basement.

"Nothing good," said Pat.

Lou glanced at the kitchen table. "Look!" he said. "Something's glittering. Is it diamonds?"

Pat bopped him on the head with the black sack. "It's glitter, you ding-dong. He looked at the floor. "There's glitter there, too. There's glitter all the way to that closet."

Pat pointed the flashlight at the pantry.

But the three friends were ready for him.

They opened the door fast. Dottie, Casey, and Leon squirted glue and glitter at Pat and Lou's faces.

Miss Grace threw confetti.

"I can't see! I can't see!" yelled Lou. "My eyes are stuck."

Pat and Lou tried to rub the glue and glitter away from their eyes.

Dottie, Casey, and Leon took the tasseled trumpet, silver horn, and metal cowbell out of their pockets. They blew and clanged their noisemakers as loud as they could.

Pat and Lou were still rubbing their eyes. They didn't know what was making all the noise.

"What is that?" asked Pat.

"It's the cops!" yelled Lou.

"Let's get out of here," yelled Pat.

They stumbled out the back door.

"I got my eyes open," yelled Pat. "Follow me."

"Are you all right?" Miss Grace asked the three friends.

"We're fine," said Dottie.

"Just a little covered with glitter and glue," said Leon.

"Do we look as glittery as you do?" asked Casey.

"You look pretty glittery," said Miss Grace.

"So do you," said Dottie.

Dottie, Casey, and Leon shook their heads. Glitter rained down from their hair onto the floor.

"Come on," said Miss Grace. "It may not be midnight yet, but we need to tell Officer Gill about the burglars. And I want to tell everyone how brave you three glitterbugs are."

CHAPTER NINE

CAUGHT!

Dottie got to her house first. Miss Grace came right behind her. Casey was third. Leon, as always, came last.

Dottie opened the door and walked inside. But as soon as she stepped into the front hall she stopped.

She stood facing a man in a suit who was wearing a burglar's mask!

"More cat burglars!" Dottie said.

"I'm so glad to see you," said Miss Grace to the masked man.

"Miss Grace, are you a cat burglar after all?" asked Casey.

Miss Grace laughed.

The masked man laughed, too. Then he took off his mask.

It was Officer Gill!

"Why are you wearing a burglar's mask?" Casey asked him.

Officer Gill looked at his mask. "This was the only mask I could find at the last minute," he said. "I didn't realize it was a burglar's mask."

Casey looked around. "Why is everyone wearing a mask?" she asked.

"Didn't you know this was a masked ball?" asked Miss Grace. She reached into her pocket and took out her invitation. She gave it to Leon.

He read it out loud. "Please come to our New Year's Eve Masked Ball."

"I brought a mask, too," Miss Grace told Officer Gill. "But I left it in my bag."

"Is that why you have a cat burglar mask in your bag?" asked Casey. "Because of the masked ball?"

"Did you think Miss Grace was a cat burglar?" asked Officer Gill.

The three friends nodded.

"We had good reasons to think that," said Leon.

"Do you want to hear them now or after we tell you about the real cat burglars?" asked Casey.

Officer Gill stopped laughing.

"What real cat burglars?" he asked. He took his notebook out of his pocket.

Dottie took her notebook out of her pocket.

"Can you tell me exactly what happened?" asked Officer Gill.

"We can show you exactly what they were going to do," said Casey.

Dottie, Casey, and Leon led Officer Gill upstairs to Dottie's room.

Dozens of purses were laid out on the

bed.

"They were going to take all those purses," Dottie said.

Suddenly, Leon's eyes grew wider.

Dottie noticed. "Leon, are you okay?"

"What is it, Leon?" Casey asked. "Did you find a rock?"

Leon shook his head. He pointed at the bed.

Everyone looked. Everyone saw.

Sticking out at the edge of the pile of coats was a pair of big black boots covered with glitter. And the pile of coats next to the glittery boots was moving!

The cat burglars were under the coats!

"Let's go downstairs and show everyone the rock you just found," said Officer Gill. He winked to let them know he saw the boots, too. He motioned for them to leave.

"Okay," said Leon.

Dottie, Casey, and Leon ran down the

stairs as fast as they could.

Officer Gill waited a moment until he knew they were safe.

Then they heard him call out, "Police. Everybody freeze!"

CHAPTER TEN

FIGURING IT OUT

Dottie, Casey, and Leon found
their parents in the dining room.

"Are you all right?" their parents asked
together.

"We're fine," Dottie said.

"You're brave," said Miss Grace.

They heard a walkie-talkie. Officer Gill

came down the stairs. The cat burglars wore handcuffs. But they were still arguing.

"I told you I was too tall for that bed," said Pat.

"It was your idea to hide under the coats," said Lou.

They were interrupted by the sound of a siren.

A police cruiser pulled up in front of the house. Its red lights flashed in the dark.

Officer Gill opened the door and led the burglars outside.

"Happy New Year," he called as he closed the door behind him.

Mrs. Plum turned back to Dottie.

"What happened?" she asked.

Everyone crowded around to hear.

Dottie told how they had discovered the cat burglars in Casey's backyard.

"Why were you outside?" asked Mrs. Calendar.

"We thought Miss Grace was the Fruitvale Cat Burglar," Leon explained. "We were coming to tell you."

"What made you think that?" asked Mr. Spector.

"Remember when I said you move as quietly as a cat?" Casey asked Miss Grace.

"Yes," said Miss Grace. "That's because I'm a gymnast. Did you know I just opened the Fruitvale Gymnastics School?"

"I meant to tell you all about that," said Mrs. Calendar. "Miss Grace is a wonderful gymnast. She can do cartwheels without using her hands."

"I'm very light on my feet," said Miss Grace. "But I never thought that would make someone think I was a cat burglar."

"It started because we saw the mask in your bag," said Dottie.

"And you're dressed all in black," said Leon.

"And we saw the diamond necklace," Dottie admitted.

"They're not really diamonds," said Miss Grace. "But I thought that necklace would look lovely with my beaded jacket."

Mrs. Plum turned to Dottie. "Why didn't you call us if you were so worried?"

"We tried," said Dottie. "But the phone didn't work."

"That was my fault," said Miss Grace. "I was about to make a phone call when I heard a noise. I put the phone down to check it out. I guess I forgot to hang it up again. I'm sorry."

"That's okay," said Dottie.

"What about my jade cupid?" asked Casey. "Did you take it?"

"Yes," said Miss Grace.

The three friends looked at one another.

"I put it in the kitchen cabinet. I didn't think you'd want it to get messy from all the glue and glitter," explained Miss Grace.

"Why were you reading *Stealing for Fun*?" asked Casey.

Miss Grace laughed. "It's a wonderful mystery. And I love mysteries. Don't you?"

"Yes," Dottie, Casey, and Leon admitted together.

"I guess that explains everything," said Mrs. Calendar.

"Almost," said Dottie. She turned to Miss Grace. "It doesn't explain why you wanted to keep us away from the windows."

Leon and Casey nodded. They wanted to know about that, too.

Miss Grace seemed surprised. She looked at Mrs. Plum. "Do you think maybe we should tell them now?" she asked.

"Tell us what?" asked Casey.

"Come with me," said Mrs. Plum.

Dottie, Casey, and Leon followed Mrs. Plum into the living room.

CHAPTER ELEVEN
SURPRISE!

"**Dottie,**" said Mrs. Plum. "Could you please turn on the light?"

"Why is it so dark in your living room?" asked Casey.

Dottie walked into the living room and turned on the light.

"Surprise!" yelled all the neighbors and relatives standing behind her.

Dottie was confused.

"Look!" said Leon. He pointed to a banner strung across the back wall.

It said, **Happy Birthday, Dottie**!

"This is why I was keeping you away from the windows," explained Miss Grace. "So you wouldn't see the sign."

"Miss Grace didn't want anything to ruin the surprise," explained Mr. Plum.

"We wanted to surprise you at midnight," said Miss Grace. "But it turned out to be harder to keep you from finding out the surprise than I expected."

"We didn't cooperate very well," said Dottie.

Miss Grace smiled. "That's okay. I understand." She took something out of her pocket. "This is for your birthday," she said. "Your mom told me you'd like it."

Dottie ripped open a small wrapped package. "Thanks!" she said. "I love it!" She held up a tiny new notebook to show everyone.

"I have something for you, too," said Mrs. Spector.

Leon's mother handed Dottie a gift.

It was another notebook. "I love this one, too," said Dottie.

Five more people gave Dottie new notebooks. Three people gave her pens.

Mrs. Calendar carried in a huge cake.

Dottie blew out the candles. Everyone sang *Happy Birthday*. Mrs. Calendar cut the cake.

Casey glanced over and noticed that Leon didn't look very happy.

"What's wrong?" asked Casey.

"I was just thinking about the rock I dropped in the clubhouse," said Leon. "I wonder if it's New York."

Casey turned to her mom. "Can we go to the clubhouse after we have cake?" she asked.

"Leon left a rock there that might be New York," Dottie said.

"Can we have our sleepover in the clubhouse?" Casey asked.

"Please," said Dottie. "For my birthday."

Dottie's, Casey's, and Leon's parents walked away to discuss it.

It didn't take long before they were back.

"You're lucky it's such a warm night," said Mrs. Plum.

The three friends cheered. They knew this meant their parents had decided they could stay in the clubhouse.

"You'll have to take sleeping bags and blankets with you so you don't get cold," said Mrs. Calendar.

"And I can help you gather your things," said Miss Grace.

Dottie, Casey, and Leon suddenly felt bad that they'd mistaken Miss Grace for a cat burglar.

"Someday can you tell us all about your gymnastics school?" asked Casey.

"I'd love to," said Miss Grace.

They all ate their cake. Then they gathered sleeping bags, blankets, snacks, and lanterns.

Dottie led the way to the clubhouse. As soon as they got there, they started searching for Leon's rock.

"There it is!" said Leon. He picked up the rock. He examined it by the light of the lantern.

"It looks exactly like New York!" he said.

"I can't wait to see what it looks like on your map," said Dottie.

After a while, Dottie, Casey, and Leon got very sleepy.

They arranged their sleeping bags and climbed inside.

At midnight, a huge cheer came from inside Dottie's house. Friends and neighbors sang the New Year's song, *Auld Lange Syne*.

But the Calendar Clubhouse was very quiet.

Dottie, Casey, and Leon were tucked in, fast asleep.

No one had nightmares. And the only thing that was the same about their dreams was that all the dreams were happy. And everyone smiled as they slept.

The Monthly Calendar

~~~~~~ Issue Six • Volume Six ~~~~~~

DECEMBER

Publisher: Casey Calendar
Editor: Dottie Plum
Fact Checker: Leon Spector

Calendar Club Catches Cat Burglars!

The big news in Fruitvale this December was that cat burglars came to town! Calendar Club members Casey Calendar, Dottie Plum, and Leon Spector searched for clues. And they found one right on Daisy Lane!

The three friends hoped to catch the Fruitvale Cat Burglars before the year ended. But it was almost New Year's Eve. They didn't have much time.

On the last night of the year, they were stuck at Casey's house with a new babysitter. But with quick thinking, they managed to help catch the cat burglars. And they had a Happy New Year at the same time!

DOTTIE'S WEATHER BOX

There are thirty-one days in December.

This year the temperatures were on or above freezing in December on twenty days.

Last year the temperature was on or above freezing in December on ten days.

How many days in December was the temperature below freezing this year? How did you figure that out?

ASK LEON

Do you have a question about a state for Leon Spector? If you do, send it to him and he'll answer it for you.

Dear Leon,

Is there such a thing as a state muffin?

From,
I'm Hungry

Dear I'm Hungry,
Maine, Minnesota, and Massachusetts all have state muffins. But my favorite state muffin is New York's apple muffin. I'm hungry, too! I wish I could eat an apple muffin right now!

Did you know the apple muffin was adopted as New York State's muffin in 1987, after students like us convinced the governor it was a good idea?

Your friend,
Leon

AND NOW,
THE WINNING
STORY FROM
THE CALENDAR
CLUB MYSTERIES™
WRITING CONTEST . . .

Congratulations to
MRS. PATRICIA PRAGER'S
2004-2005 CLASS 3P OF
BEN FRANKLIN ELEMENTARY,
the Winners of
the Calendar Club Mysteries™
Writing Contest and authors of
THE CASE OF THE VENGEFUL VALENTINE:

Jack Amadeo	Gregory Lenane
Keith Butcher	Dakota Mascalino
Kelly Cirillo	Michael McLaughlin
Alex Cohen	Ziko McLean
Melissa Daly	Kim Monteferante
Matthew deMarte	Mike Ortiz
Jimmy Flaherty	Mihir Paradkar
Mary Golden	Mary Roselle
Marcio Guevara	Lauren Spedaliere
Alexis Hickson	Marianne Triano
Josh Kale	Pat Winton
Anthony Zegarelli	

THE CASE OF THE VENGEFUL VALENTINE

BY CLASS 3P AT BEN FRANKLIN ELEMENTARY

It was raining hard. Dottie Plum ran as fast as she could. She got to the clubhouse first.

Leon Spector arrived next. He was dripping wet because he stopped on the way to look at a rock.

They stood inside the clubhouse and waited for Casey. She had called and asked them to meet her right away. She didn't say why, but Dottie and Leon agreed — it sounded important.

After a few seconds, Casey arrived

with a big box of chocolates. The box was heart-shaped, about ten inches at the widest and longest parts. It was covered with red velvet and trimmed with lace. A large yellow ribbon was in the center of the box, on top of a piece of paper. There were musical notes written on top of the box. The musical notes were written with a black marker on the red velvet.

"Hey, what's in the box?" asked Leon.

"Chocolates!" answered Casey. "And that's what we're here to talk about."

"Can I please, please, have the first chocolate?" begged Dottie.

Casey wasn't surprised that Dottie wanted the first chocolate. Dottie always wanted to be first. Casey replied, "Yes," as she carefully lifted the lid off the box. The chocolates looked delicious. They were white, red, pink, and brown.

Dottie plucked a chocolate out of the box

and hurriedly bit into it, expecting a sweet, chocolatey taste. "Eewh! This is disgusting! I think I'm going to be sick." Dottie spit out the chocolate onto the floor. "What kind of chocolate is this?" screamed Dottie, as she grabbed the box from Casey.

"Like I said, that's why we came here," explained Casey. "I found this chocolate in my mailbox this morning when I was mailing my valentines, but it doesn't say who it's from. And I didn't know the chocolates tasted yucky. I thought it would be a good case for the Calendar Club."

"That's a great idea!" replied Leon. "Did you notice that piece of paper? And those mysterious musical notes?"

"What musical notes?" groaned Dottie, holding her stomach. "Whoever put those chocolates in your mailbox must be mad at you. They taste like soap!"

"Who could be mad at me?" wondered Casey.

"You never hurt anybody," said Leon. "Let's look at those musical notes and the paper. Maybe they're clues to help us find out who did this."

Dottie, Casey, and Leon looked at the musical notes. "They look a little familiar to me," said Leon. "Don't you think so, too? Where have we seen those notes before?"

"I'm not sure," groaned Dottie. "Let's go play them on my piano! But first, I've got to get a drink of water to get this horrible taste out of my mouth. Maybe I'll feel better then."

Leon looked out the window. "I'm glad it's not raining anymore. Now I can look for more states . . . I mean, rocks."

Dottie led the way to her house. Leon found a rock that looked just like Florida.

He put it in his pocket with the others he had collected that day.

As Dottie, Casey, and Leon entered the house, Ginger the cat ran to them. Dottie ran to the sink. Casey and Leon ran to the piano and set down the box of chocolates. Ginger followed Casey and Leon to the piano.

"That's better," sighed Dottie as she

joined Casey and Leon and Ginger at the piano. "It was weird. When I took a drink of water, little soap bubbles came out of my mouth."

"What?" cried Casey.

"Huh?" wondered Leon. "The soap bubbles must be another clue. The chocolate candy is really soap!"

"Let's get down to the music," said Dottie seriously.

As Dottie played the music it sounded familiar. "Hey, that sounds like — 'The Pumpkin Song'!" the kids all shouted together.

"It's 'The Pumpkin Song' we learned in kindergarten," Leon said.

"He's back!" Dottie shouted.

"The Pumpkin Man!" added Casey.

"I thought he was in jail," said Leon.

"Maybe he escaped!" suggested Dottie.

"Let's call Officer Gill," Casey said.

"Okay, but let's look at the note first," insisted Leon. "It says, 'Ha! Ha! Ha! H.V.D.' "

"What's H.V.D.?" wondered Dottie. "Maybe the answer is on the back of the note."

"I never looked at the back," said Casey, as she turned the note over. "Oh, no! It says, 'I'm back for revenge.' Call Officer Gill now!"

Dottie called Officer Gill and told him all about Casey's box of chocolates made out of soap, the musical notes from "The Pumpkin Song," and the note. "We think the Pumpkin Man we helped you catch in October left this for Casey."

Officer Gill said he would be right over

to look at the evidence. Just then, Casey turned on the TV. The news was on. The reporter said, "The infamous Pumpkin Man has escaped. He's headed to Fruitvale."

"Oh, no! He must already be here. Leon and I are probably next!" cried Dottie.

"Let's check our mailboxes to see if he's left anything," said Leon. "Let's see if it's raining again."

The three kids looked out the window. "Look!" cried Dottie. The kids saw a stranger in a raincoat and rain hat putting something in Dottie's mailbox.

"Caught red-handed!" shouted Leon.

"Oh, no. He's getting away," said Casey.

Right at that moment, Officer Gill pulled up in his police car. He jumped out, grabbed the stranger, put handcuffs on him, and put him in the backseat of his car. The kids rushed out. "Thank goodness you called me," said Officer Gill. "We'll put this guy back where he can't hurt anybody. You kids can come down to the police station and give me all the details."

At the police station, Casey and Dottie were talking to Officer Gill. They were waiting for Leon, who thought he had spotted a rock shaped like Illinois and another one shaped like Maine. Finally, Leon opened the door. "What a great day," said Leon. "Illinois and Maine were lying right next to each other."

"Well, it is a great day for Fruitvale," said Officer Gill, "thanks to the Calendar Club. I have a special reward for you." Officer Gill opened a closet and pulled out the biggest heart-shaped box of

chocolates the kids had ever seen. It was three feet at its longest and widest points. "Don't worry. This box has no soap!" promised Officer Gill.

"Dottie, why don't you have the first piece?" said Casey.

"Well . . . I don't know. . . . Oh, okay!" Dottie carefully lifted a dark brown chocolate out of the box and slowly placed it in her mouth. "Ahhhhhhhhh! That's more like it!"